# TUESDAY

DAVID WIESNER

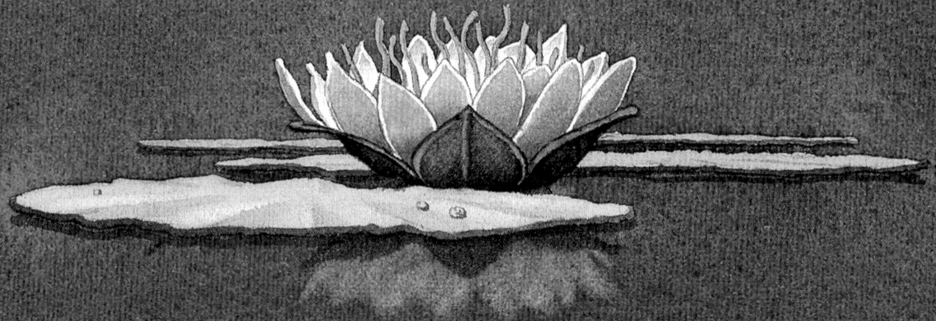

ANDERSEN PRESS

TUESDAY EVENING, AROUND EIGHT.

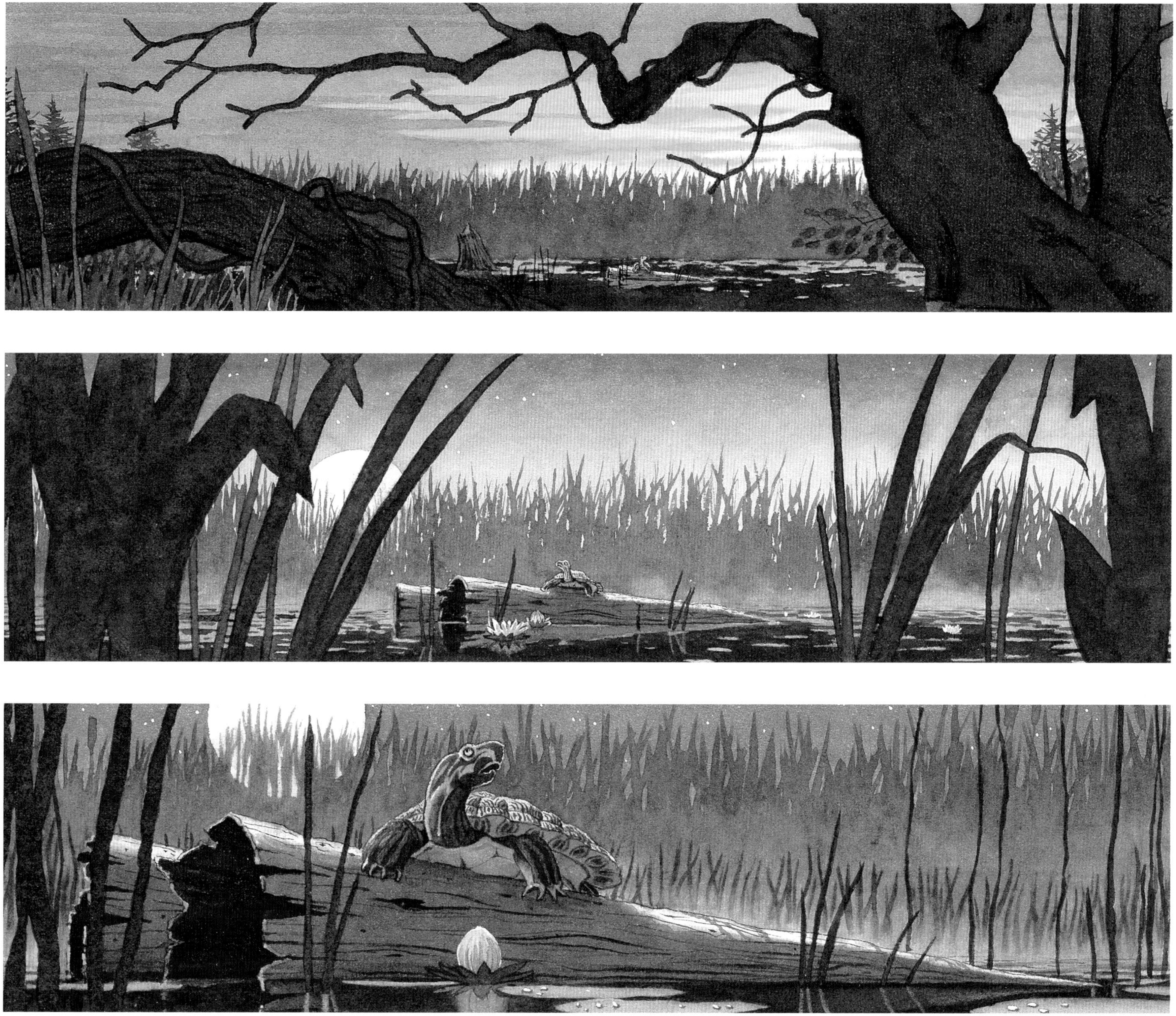

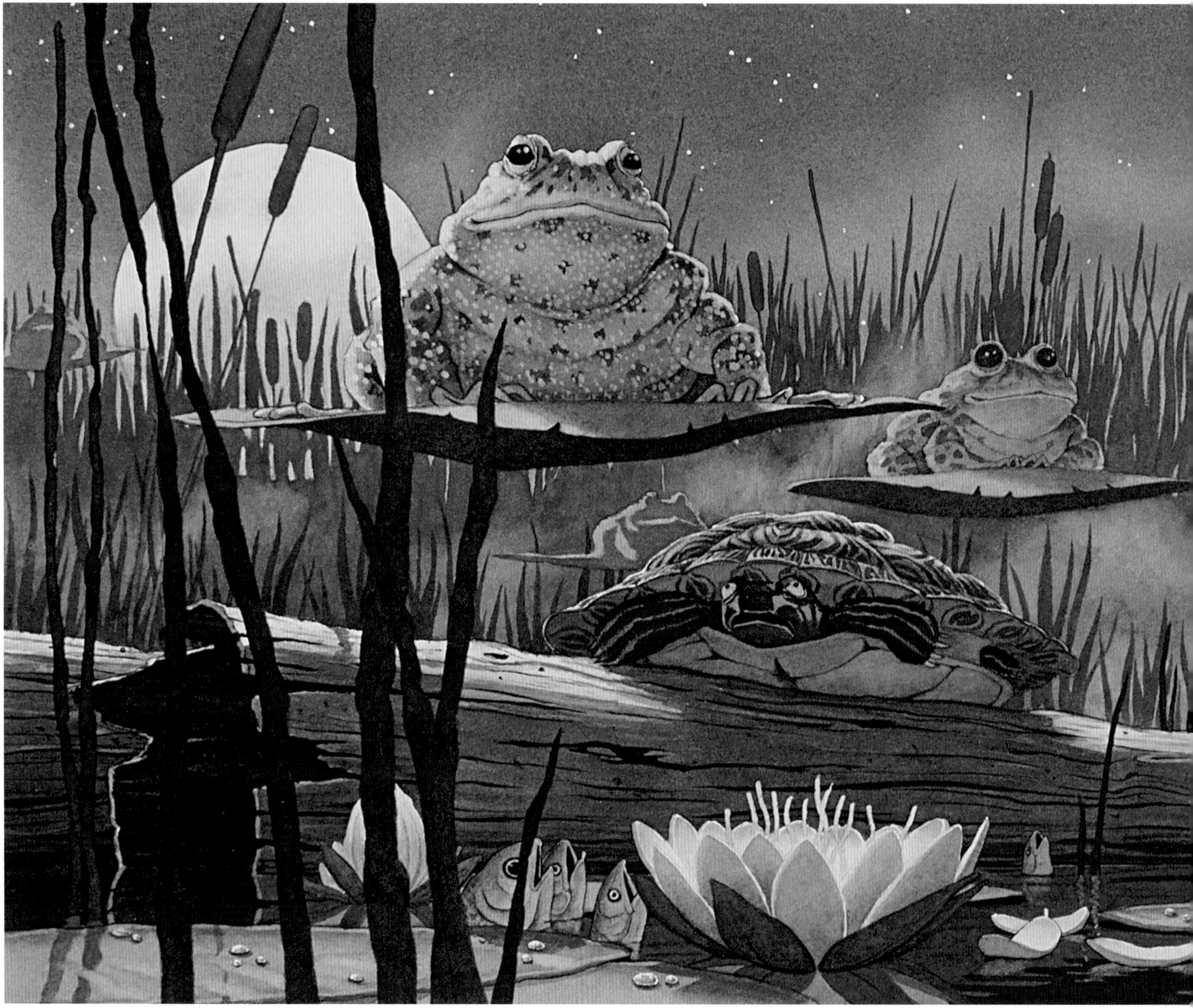

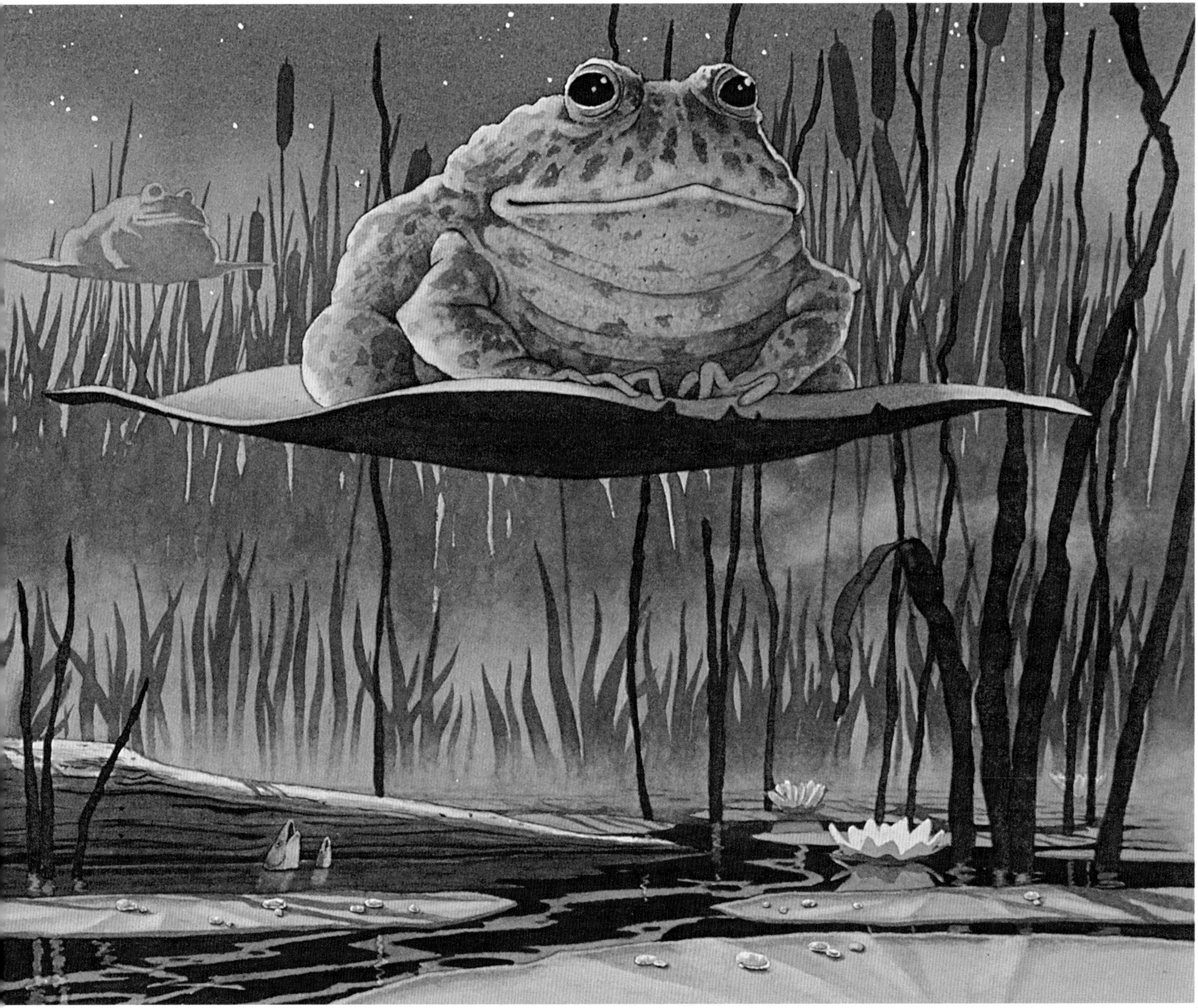

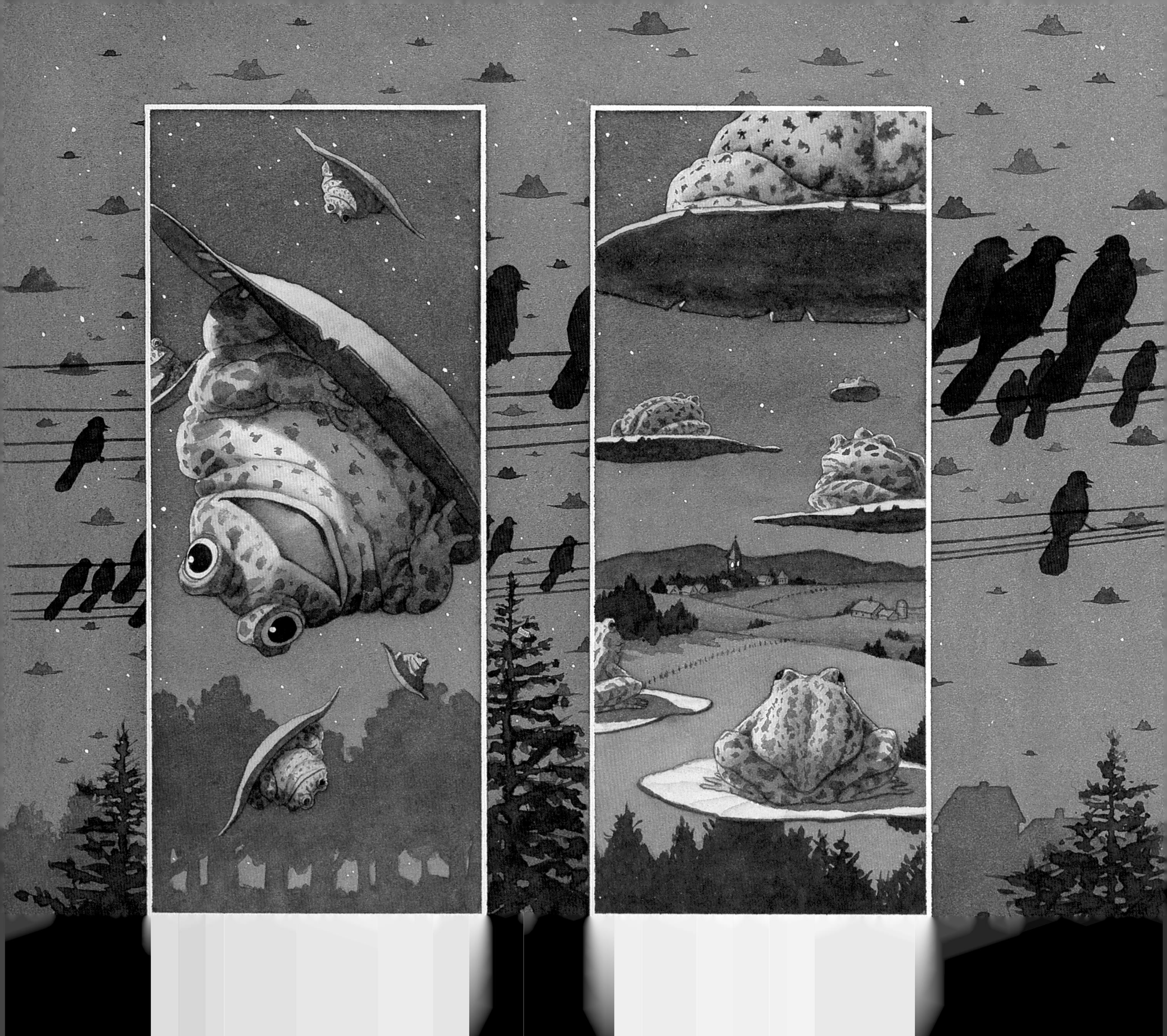

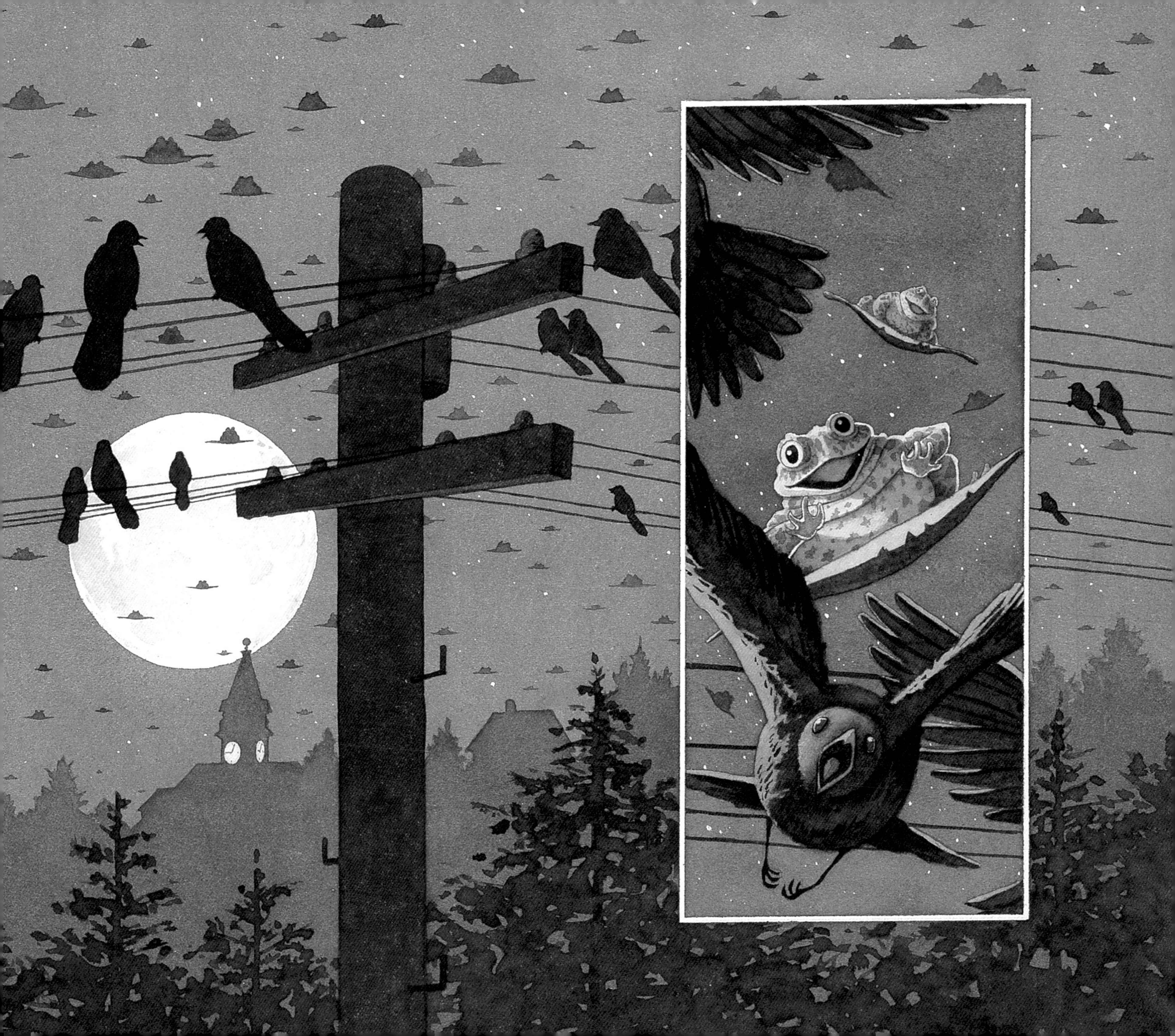

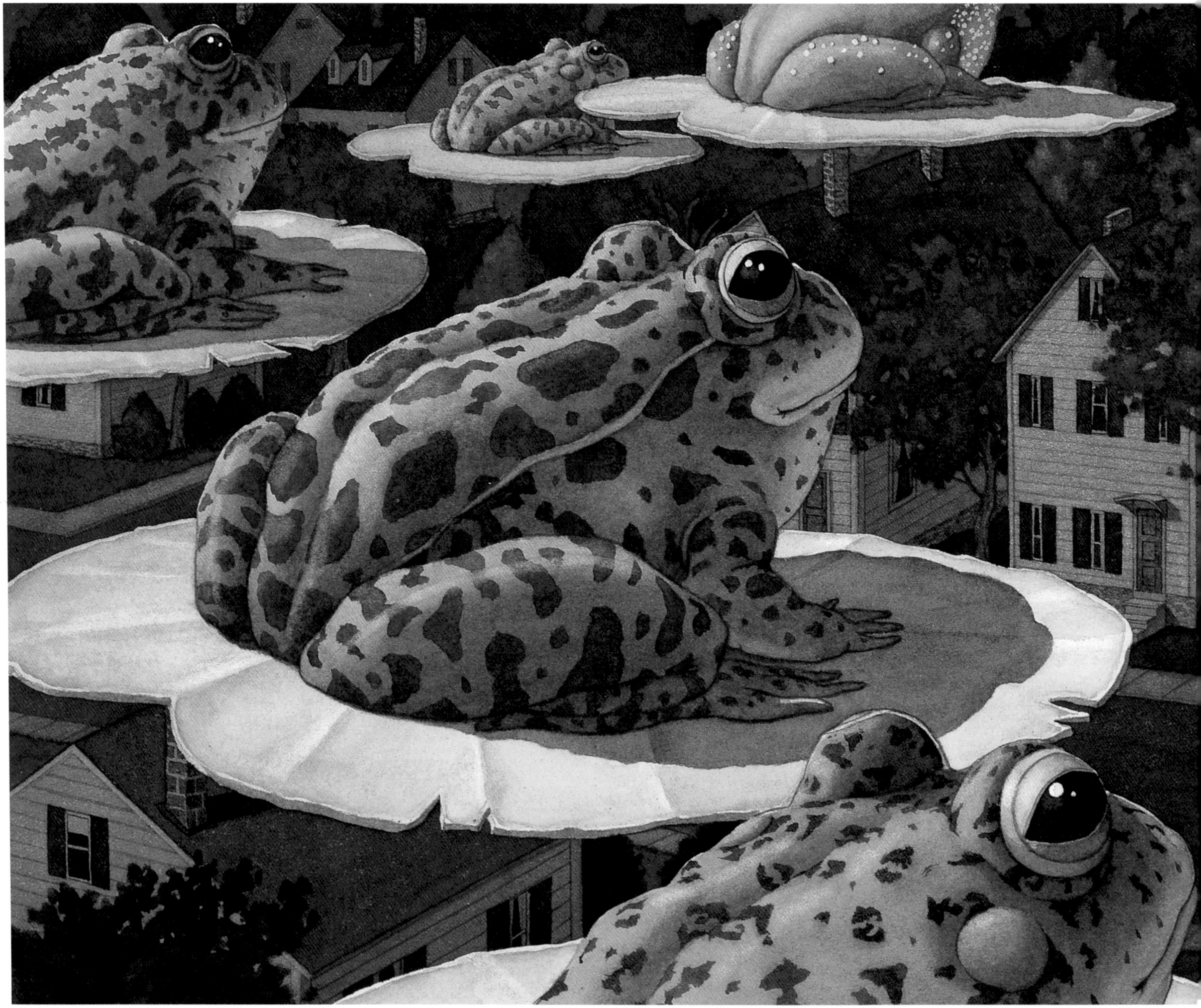

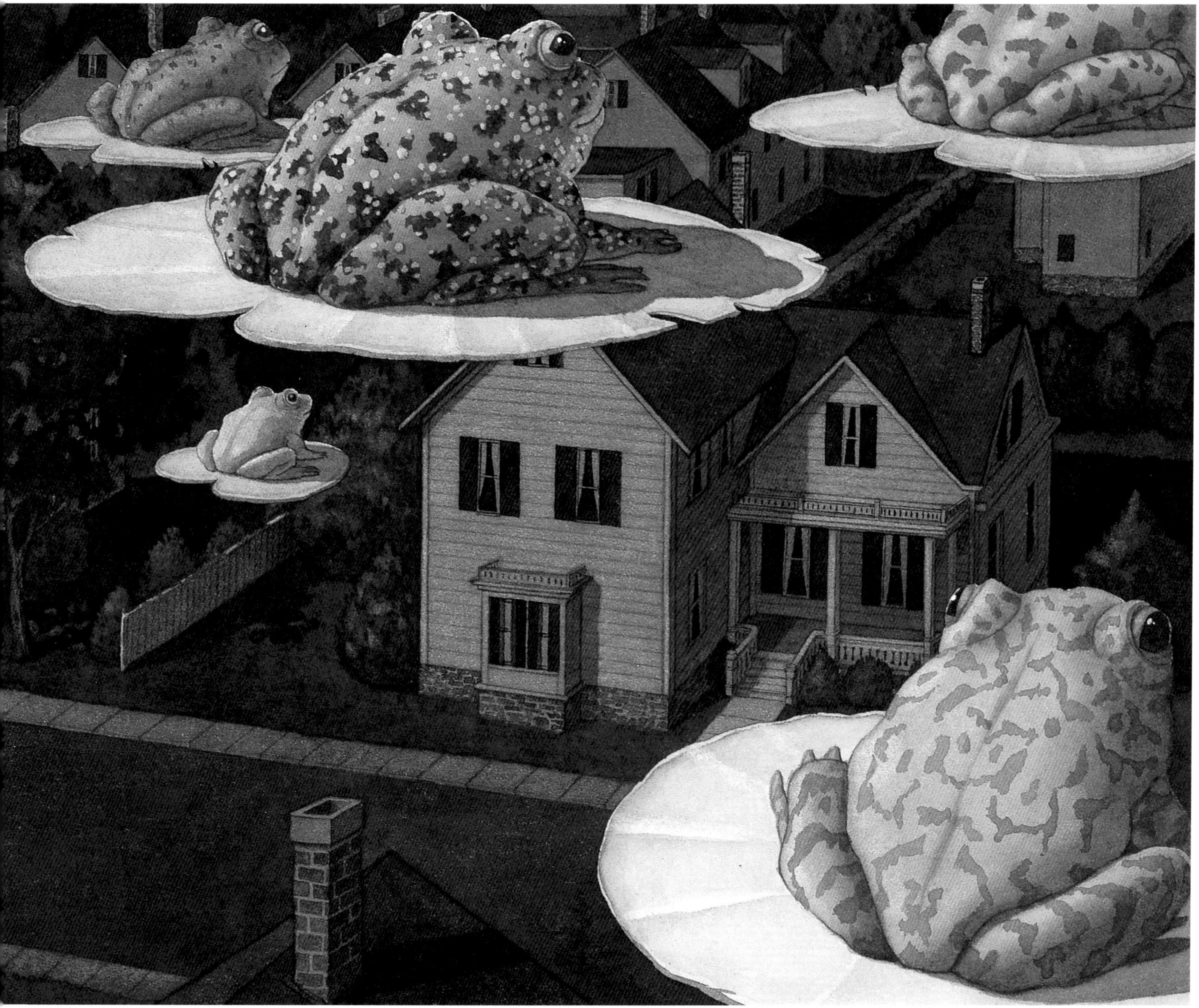

11:21 P.M.

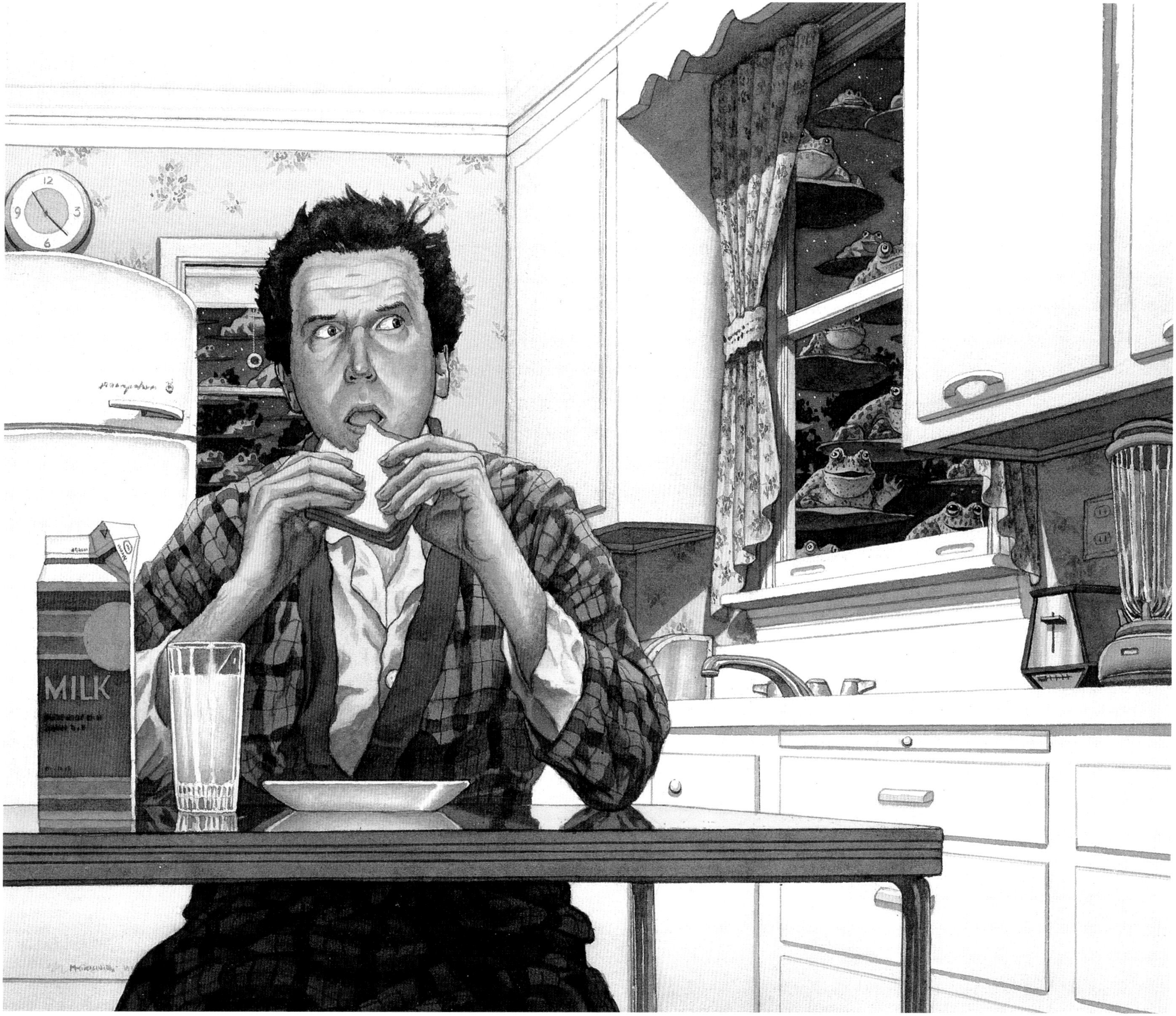
MILK

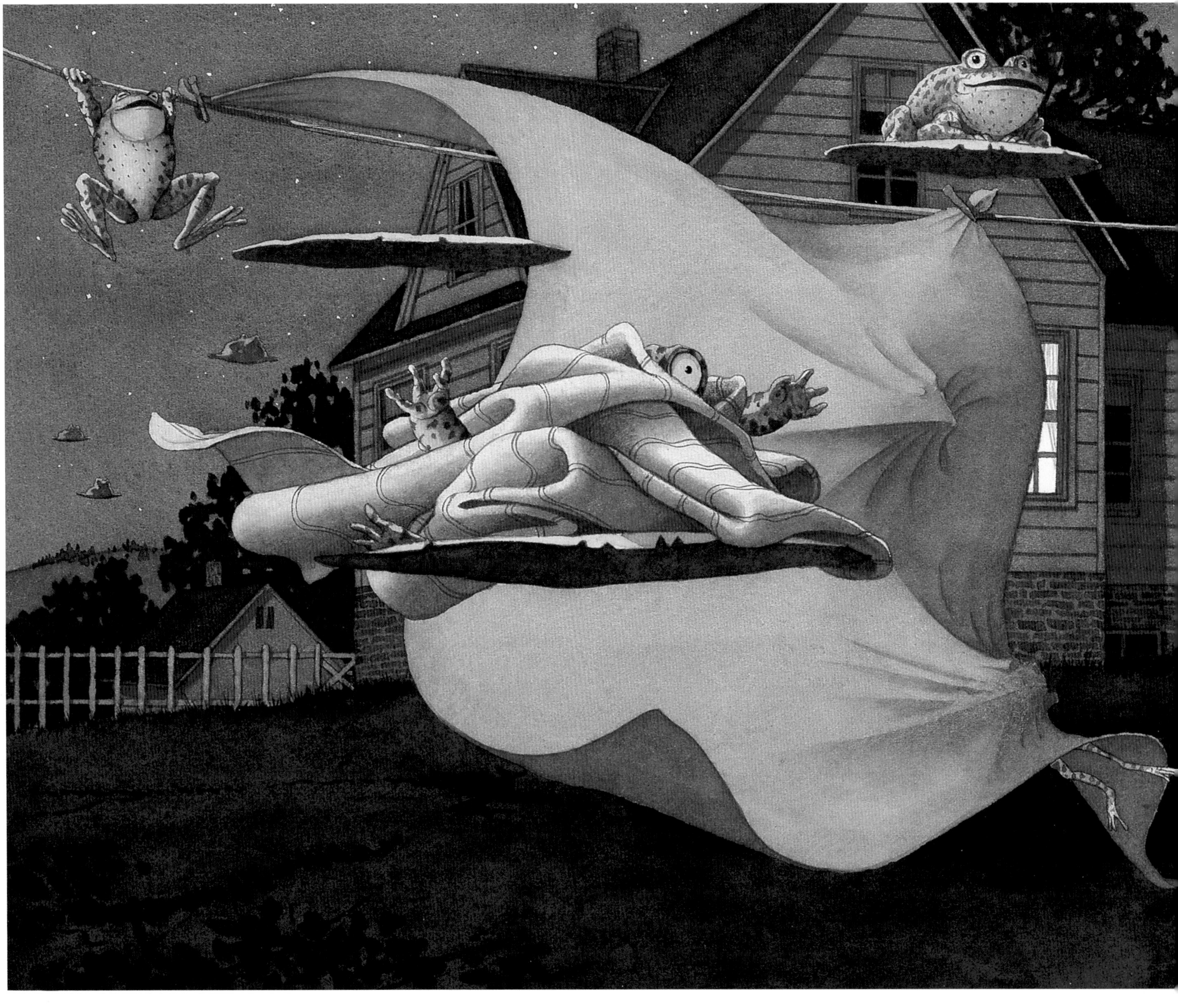

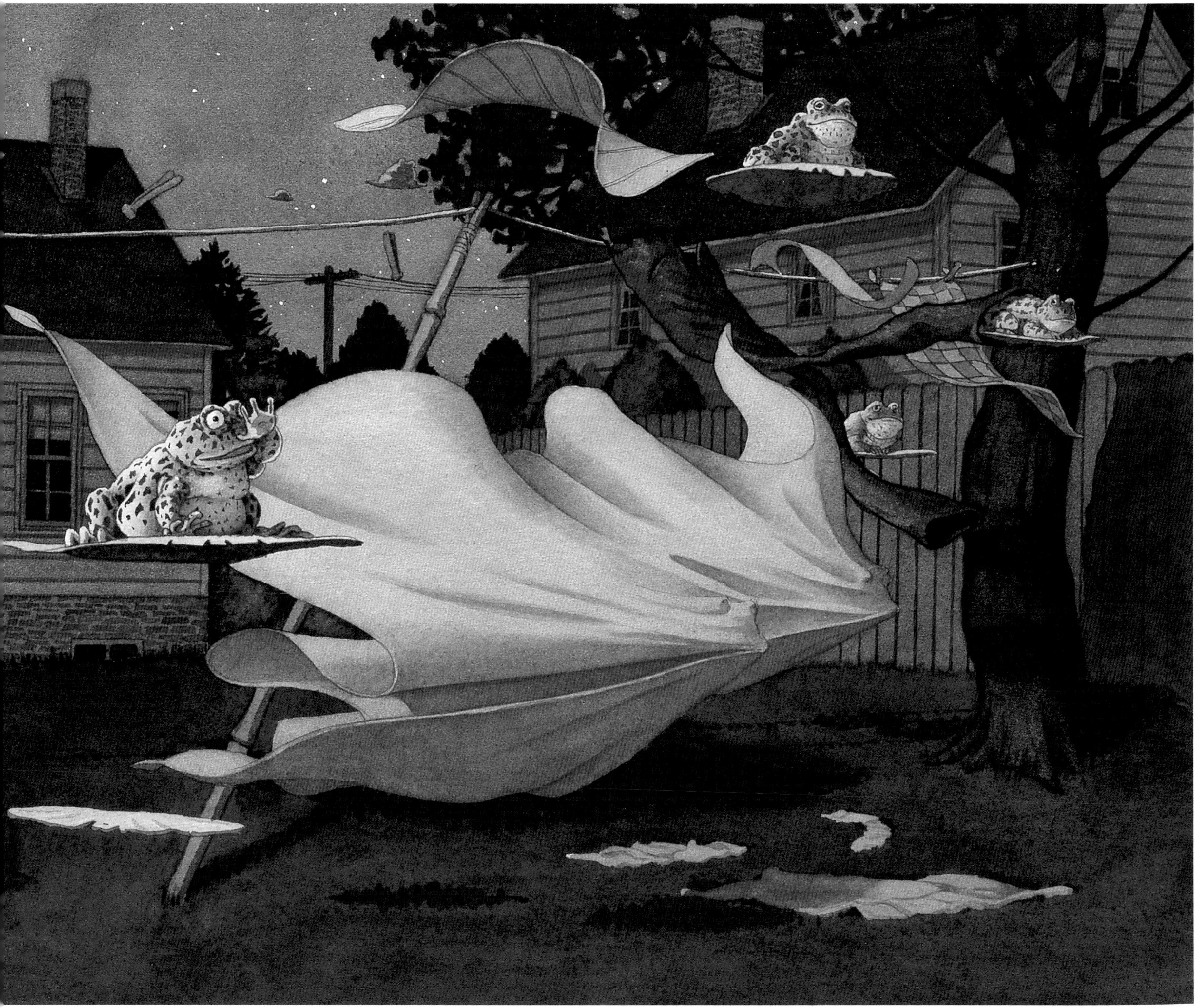

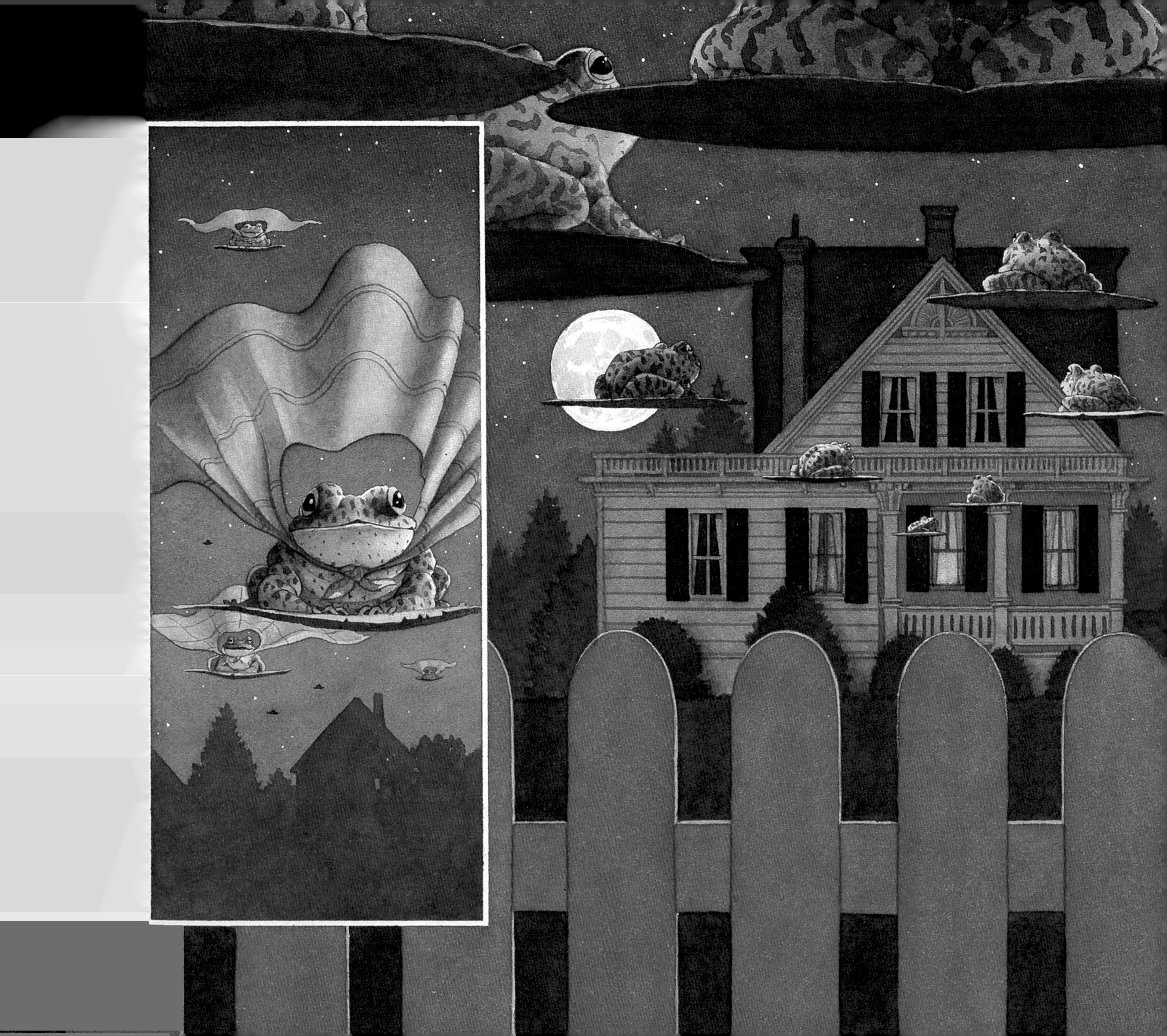

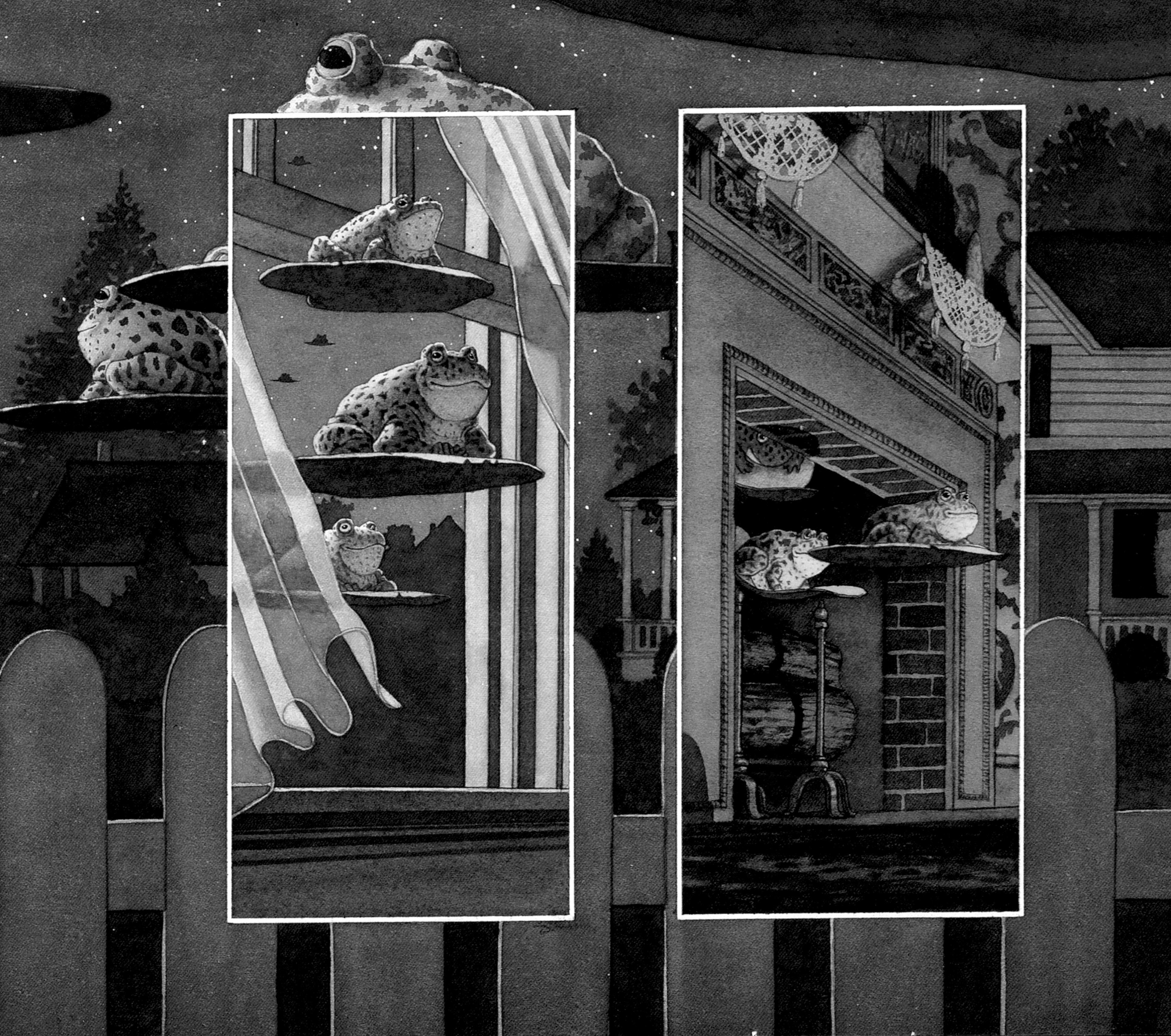

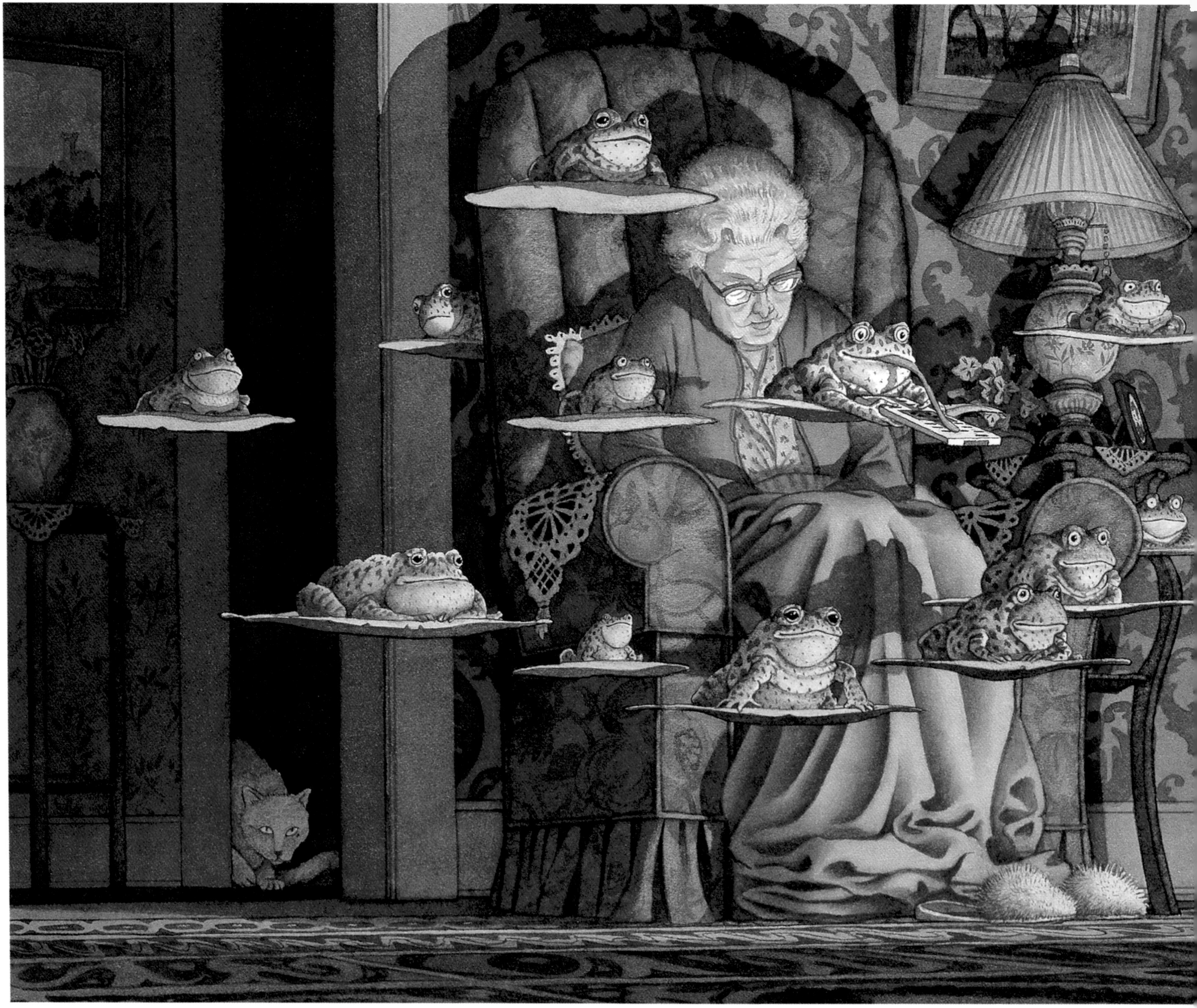

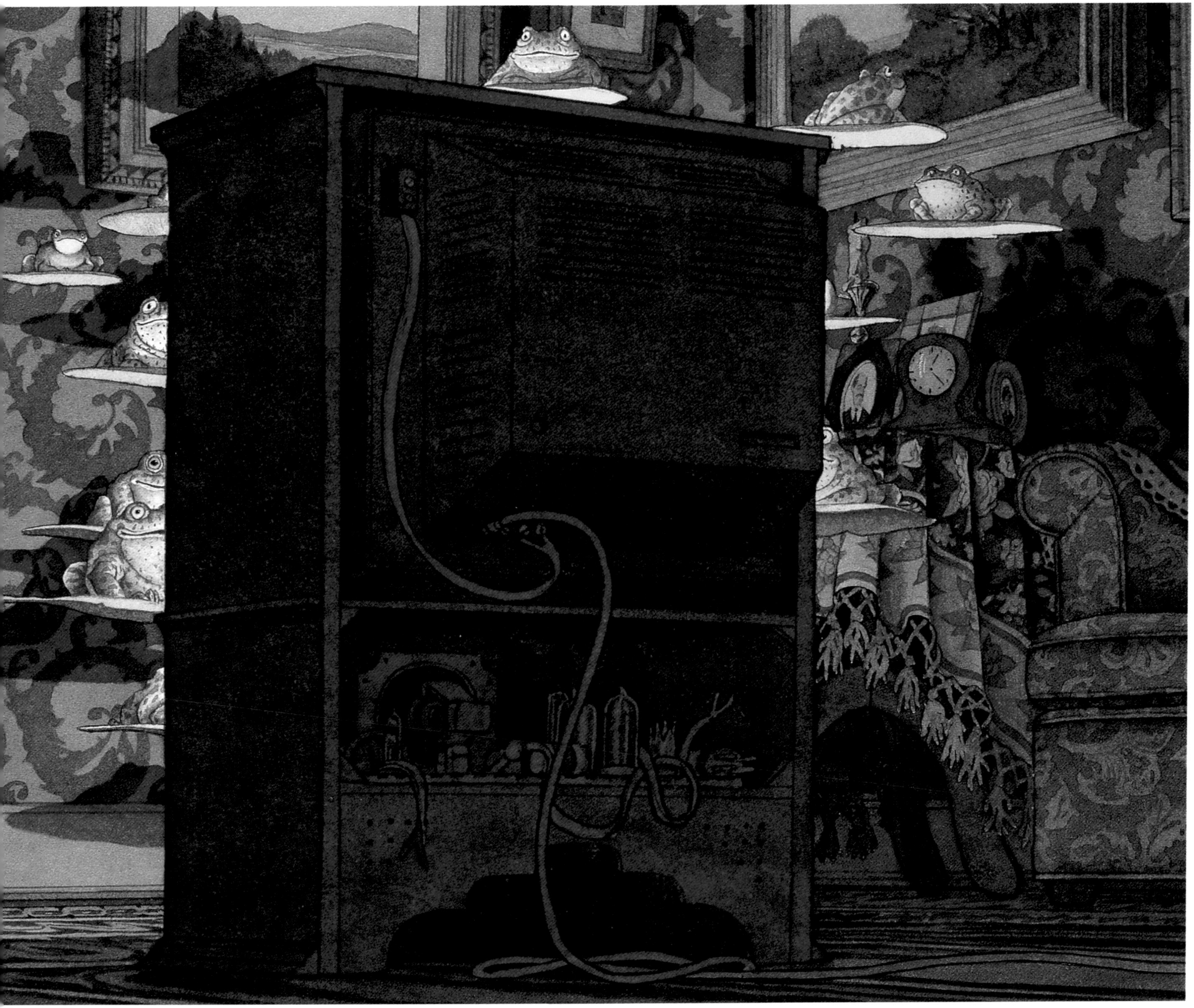

4:38 A.M.

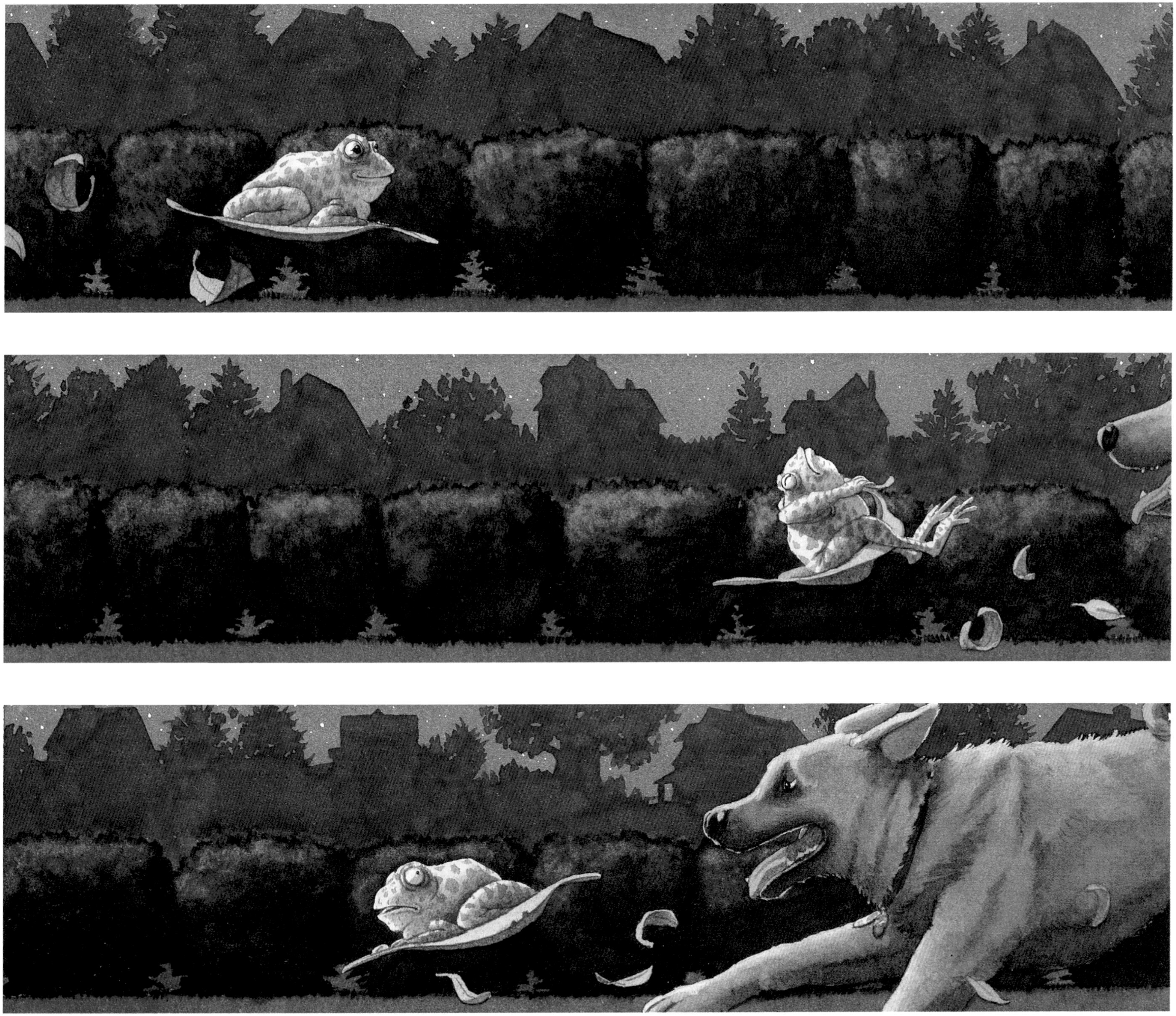

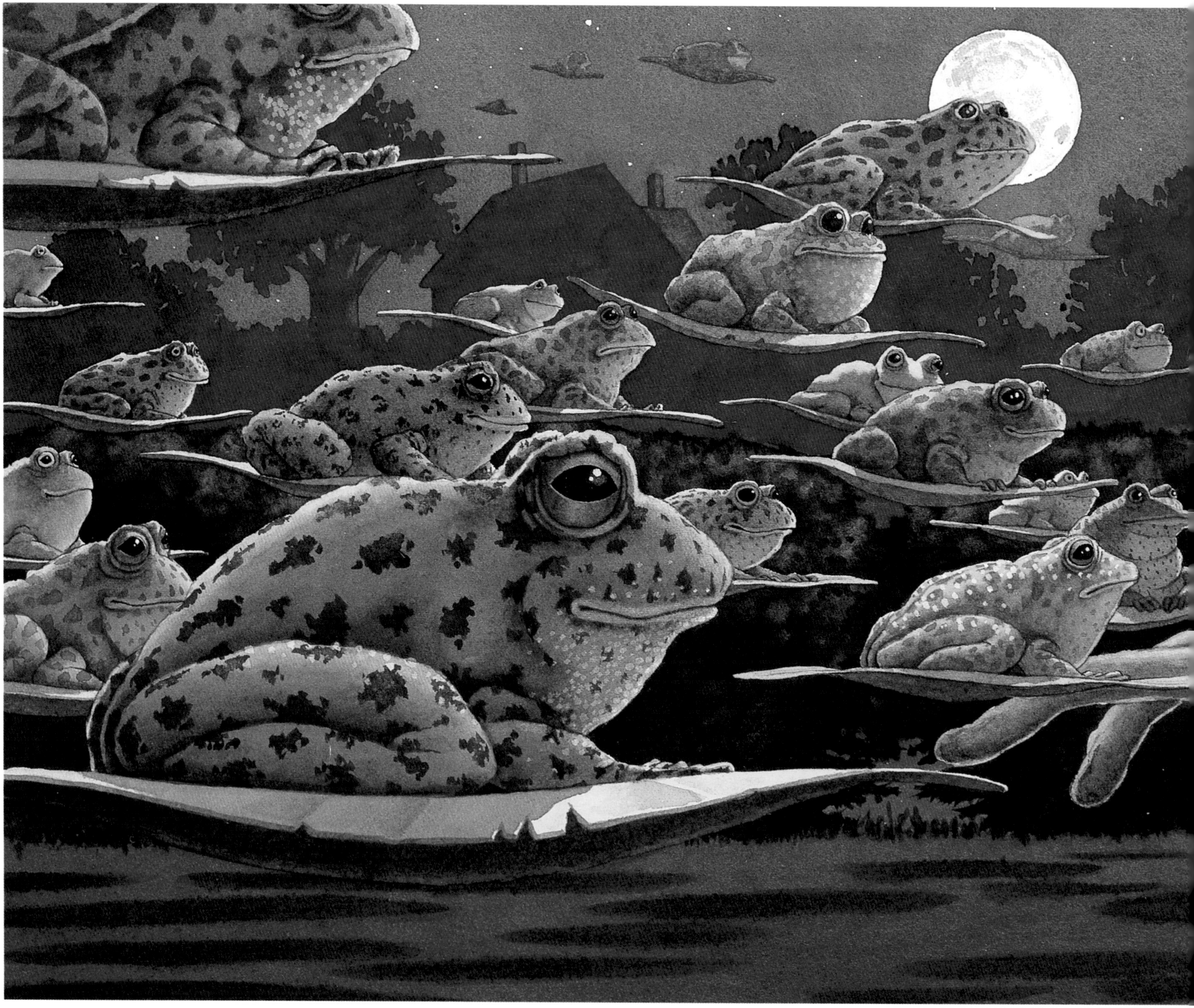

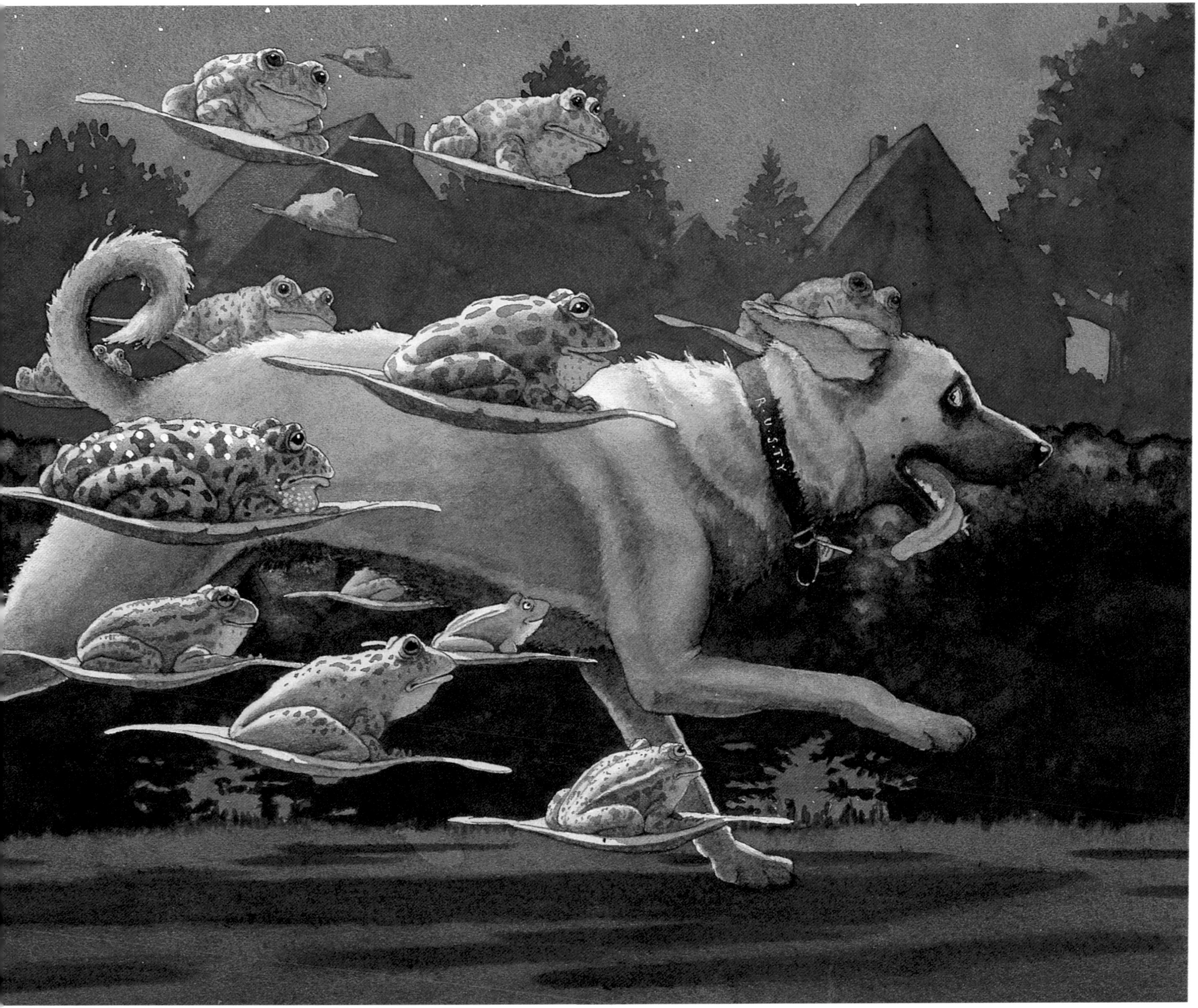
R.U.S.T.Y

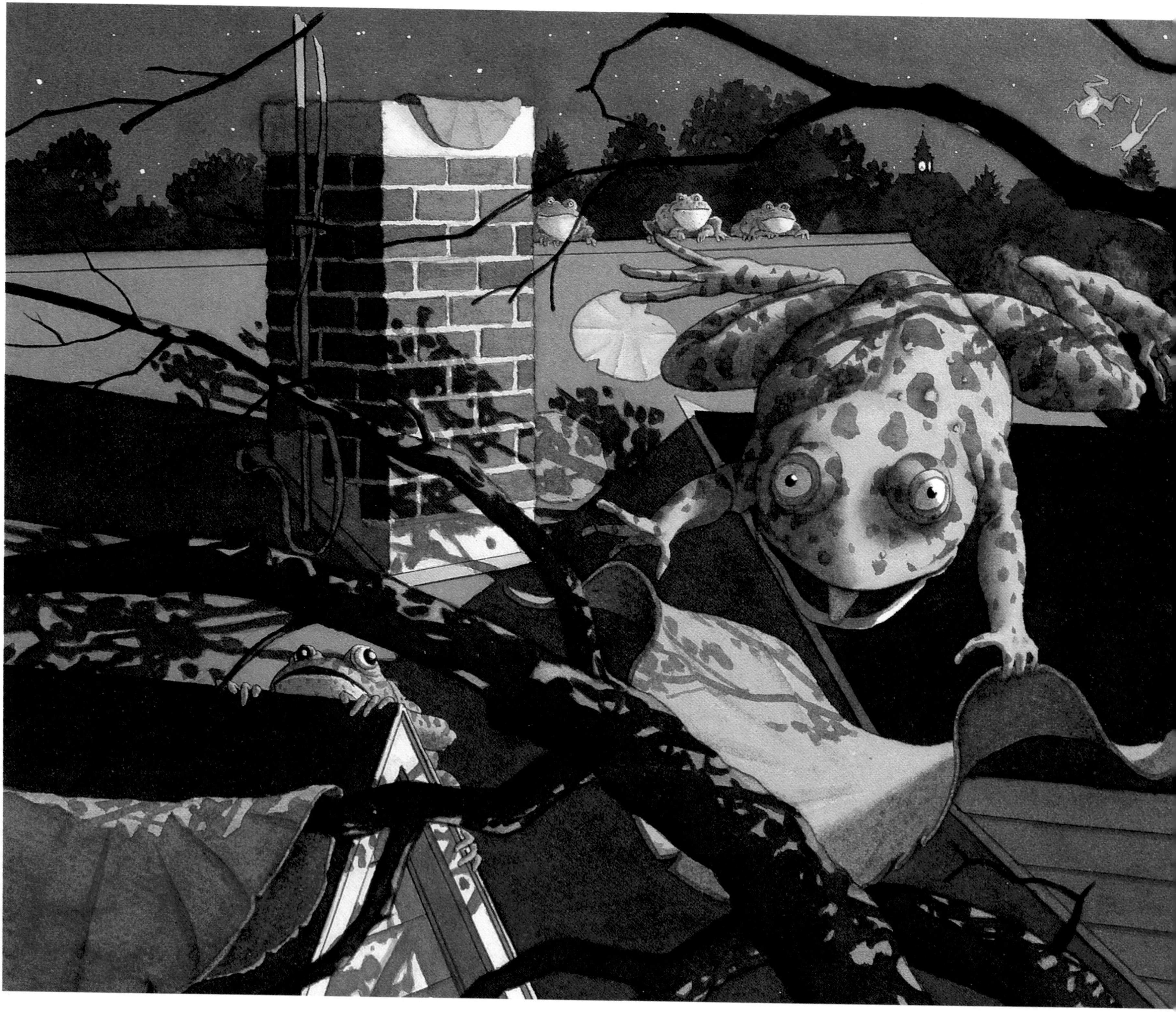

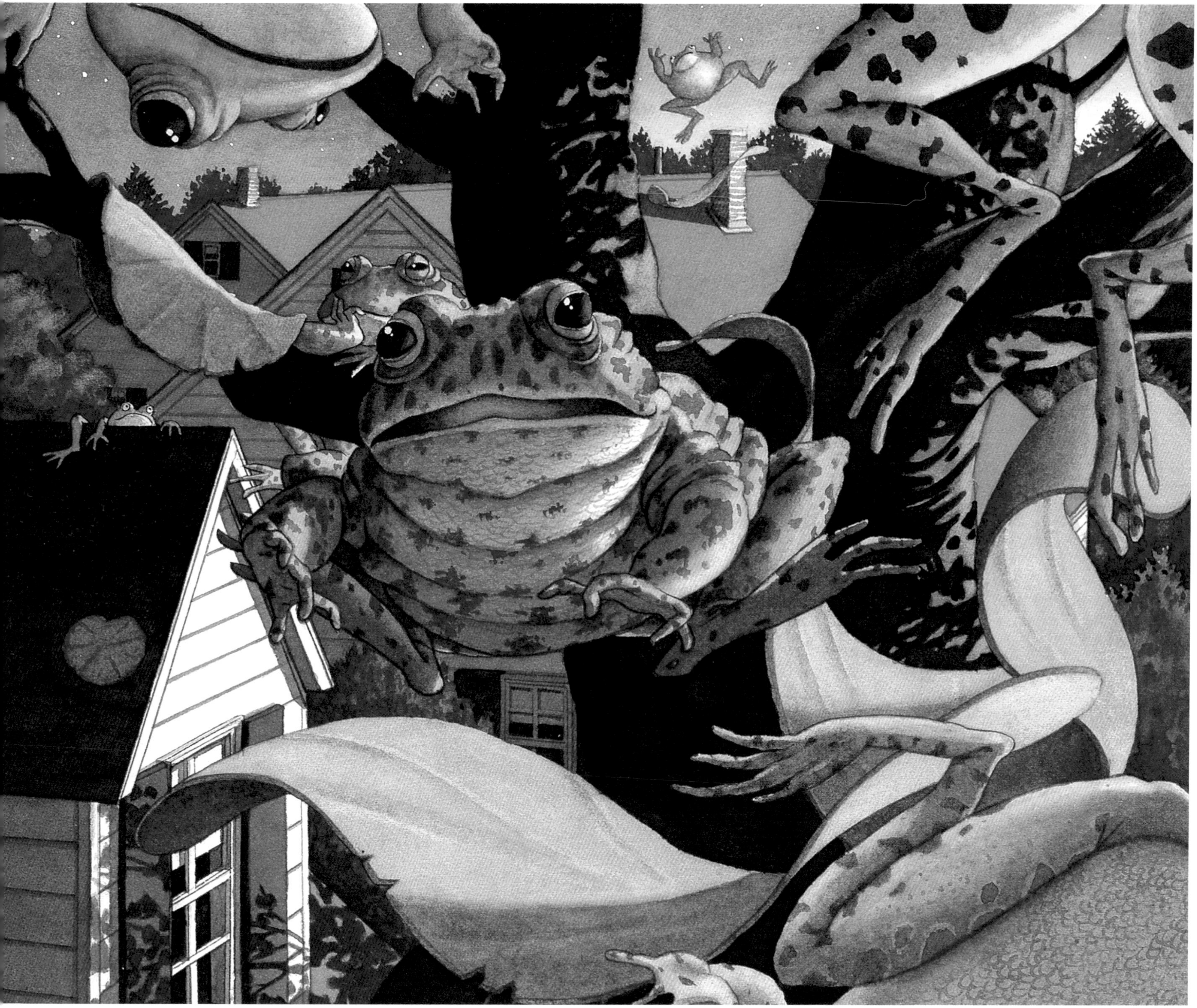

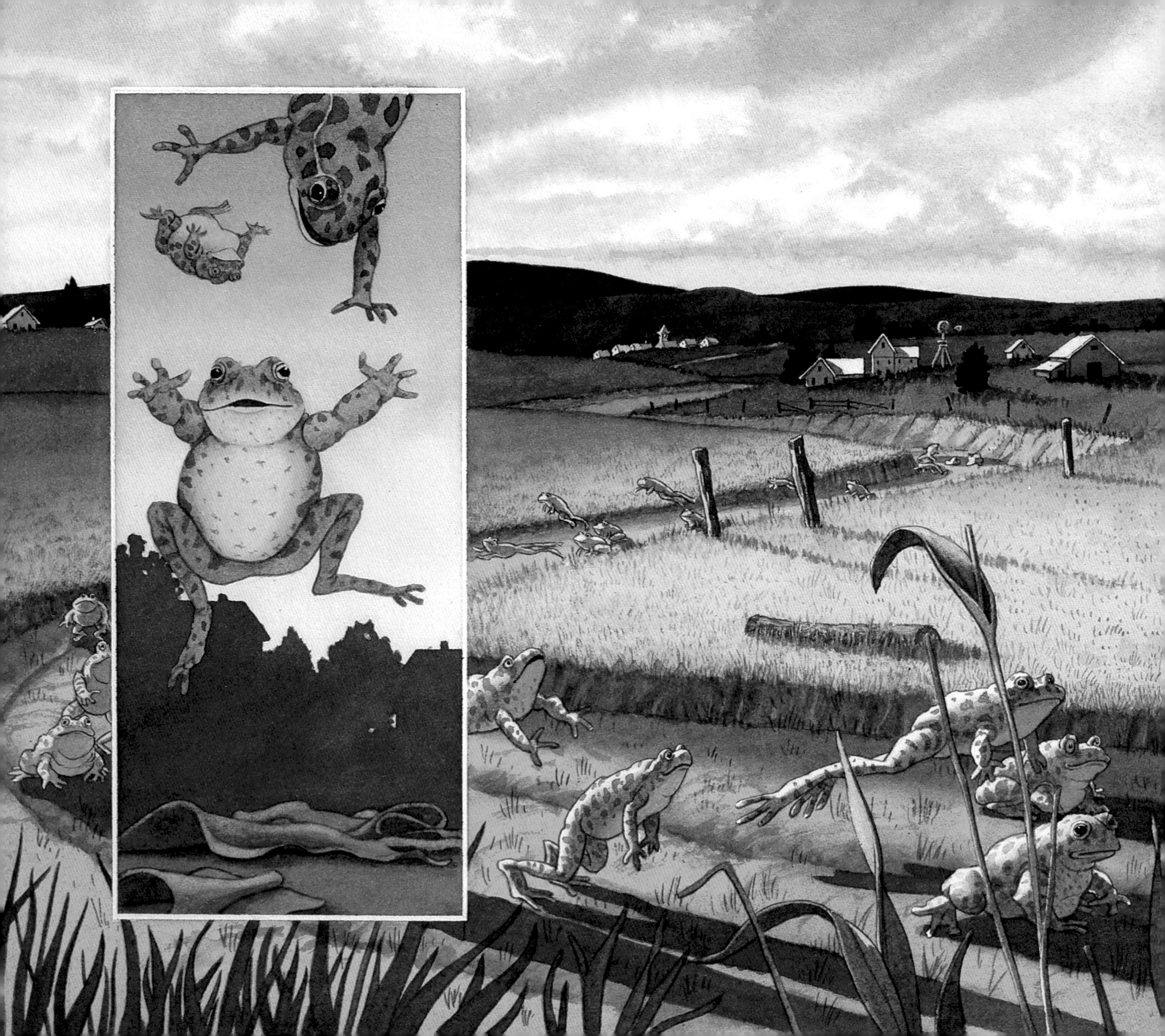

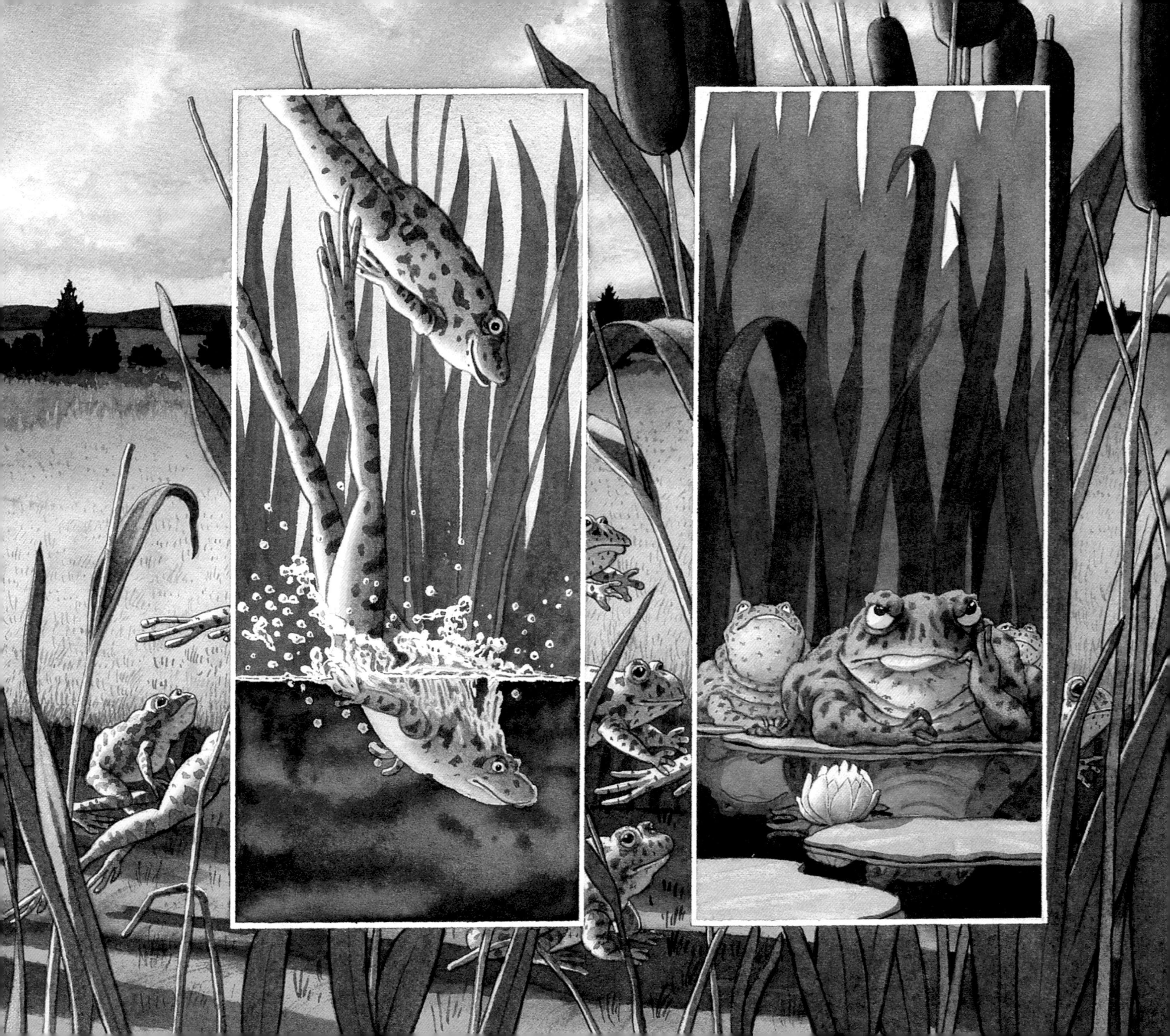

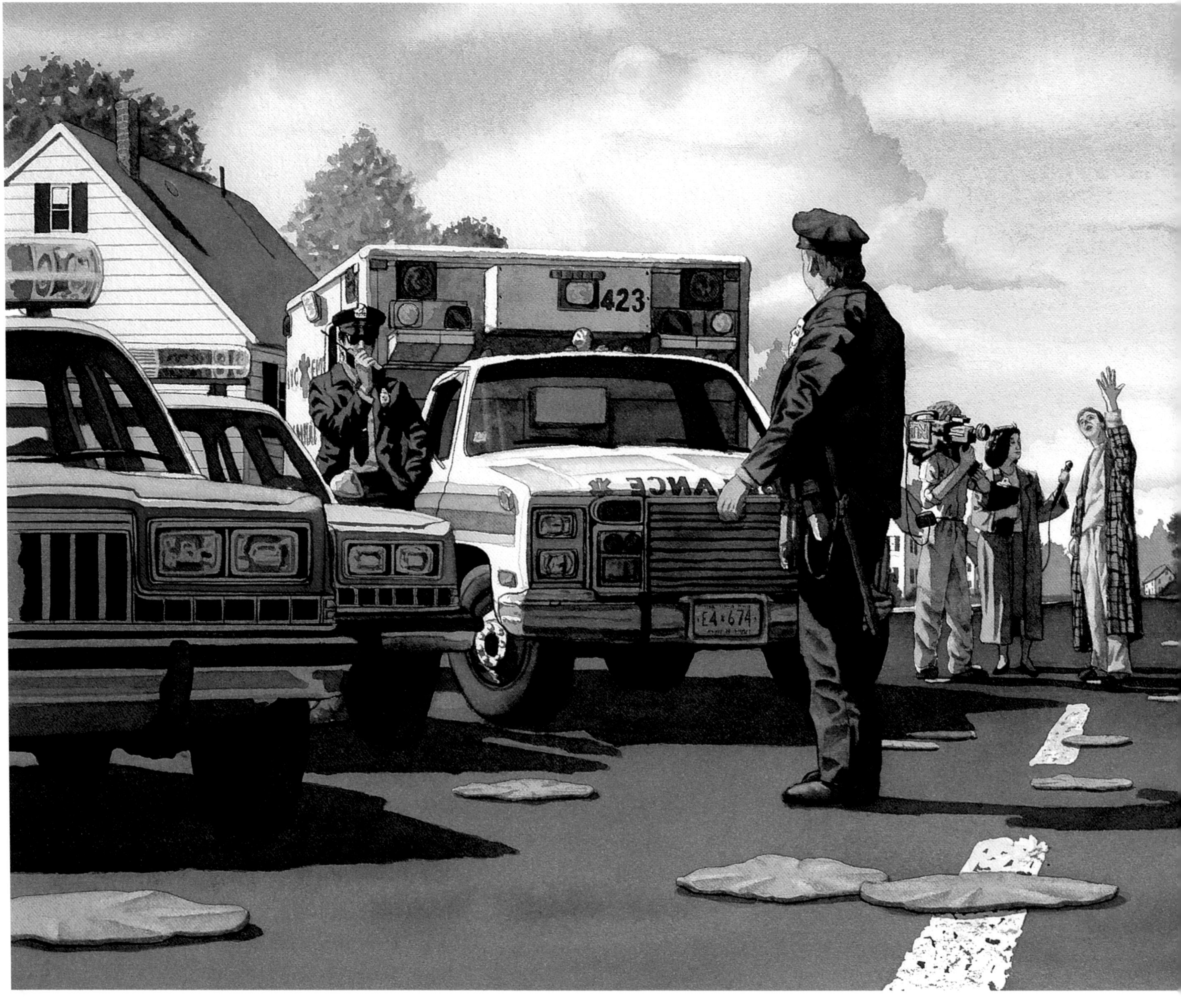
423
E4·674

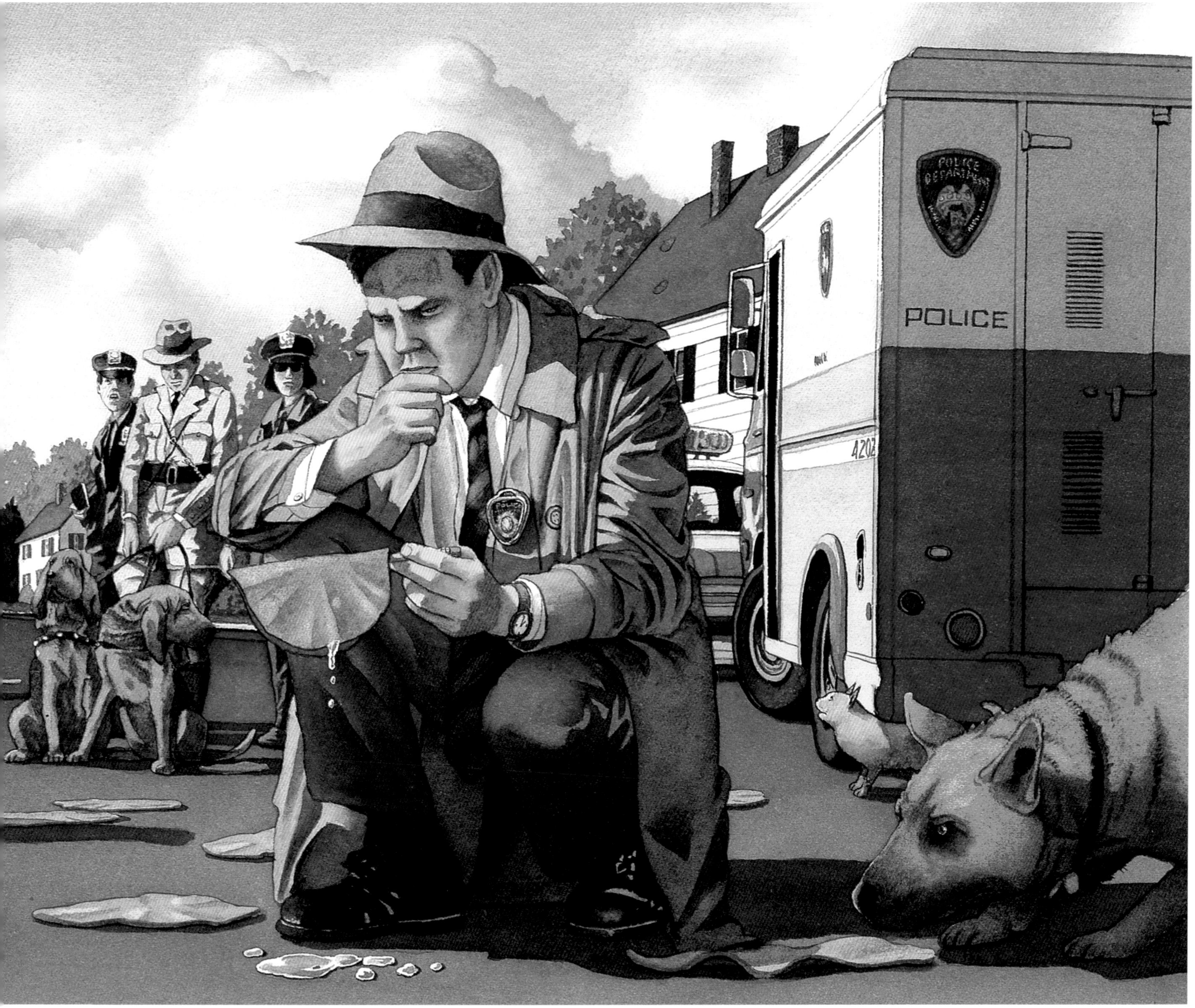
POLICE
4202

NEXT TUESDAY, 7:58 P.M.

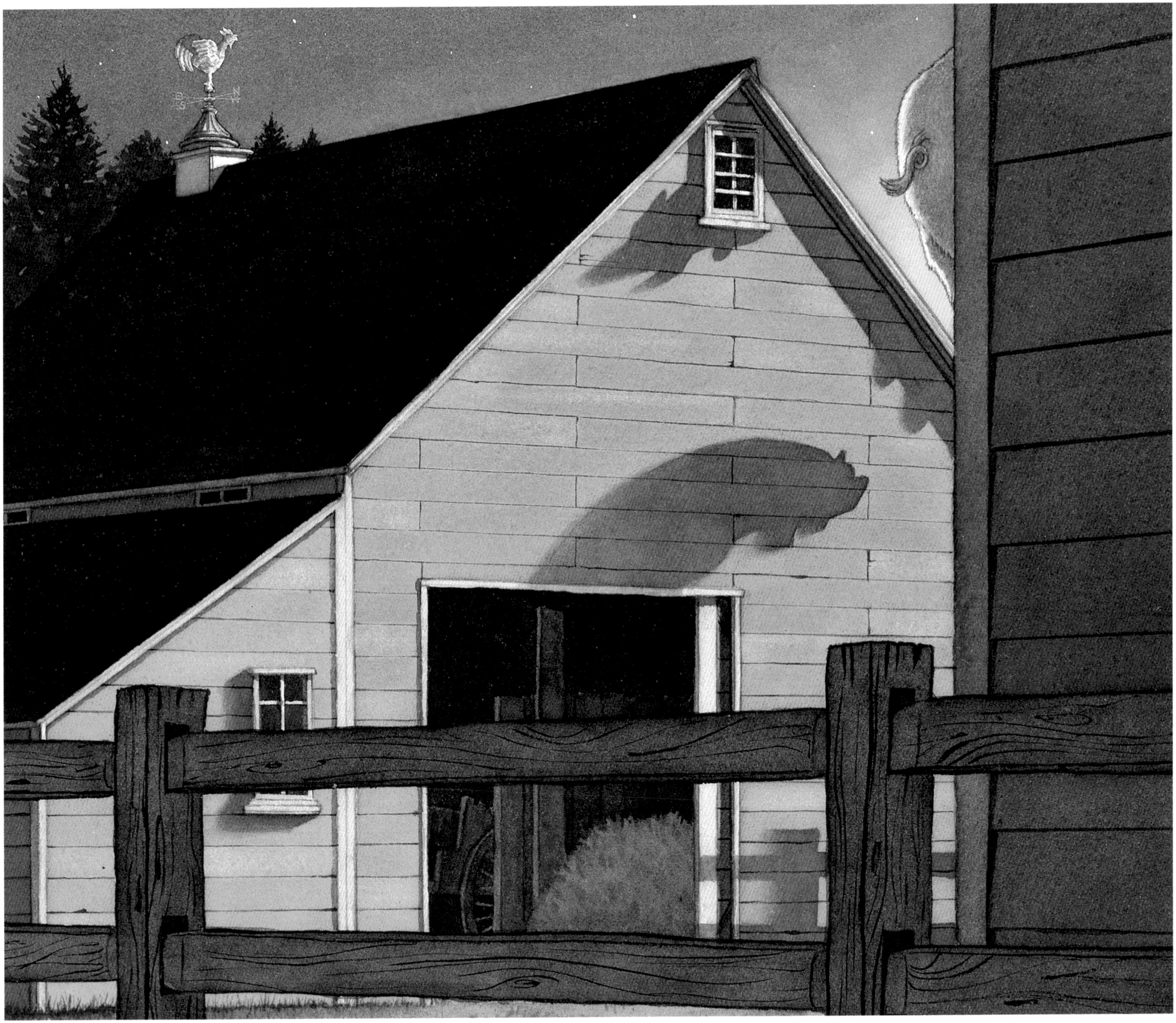

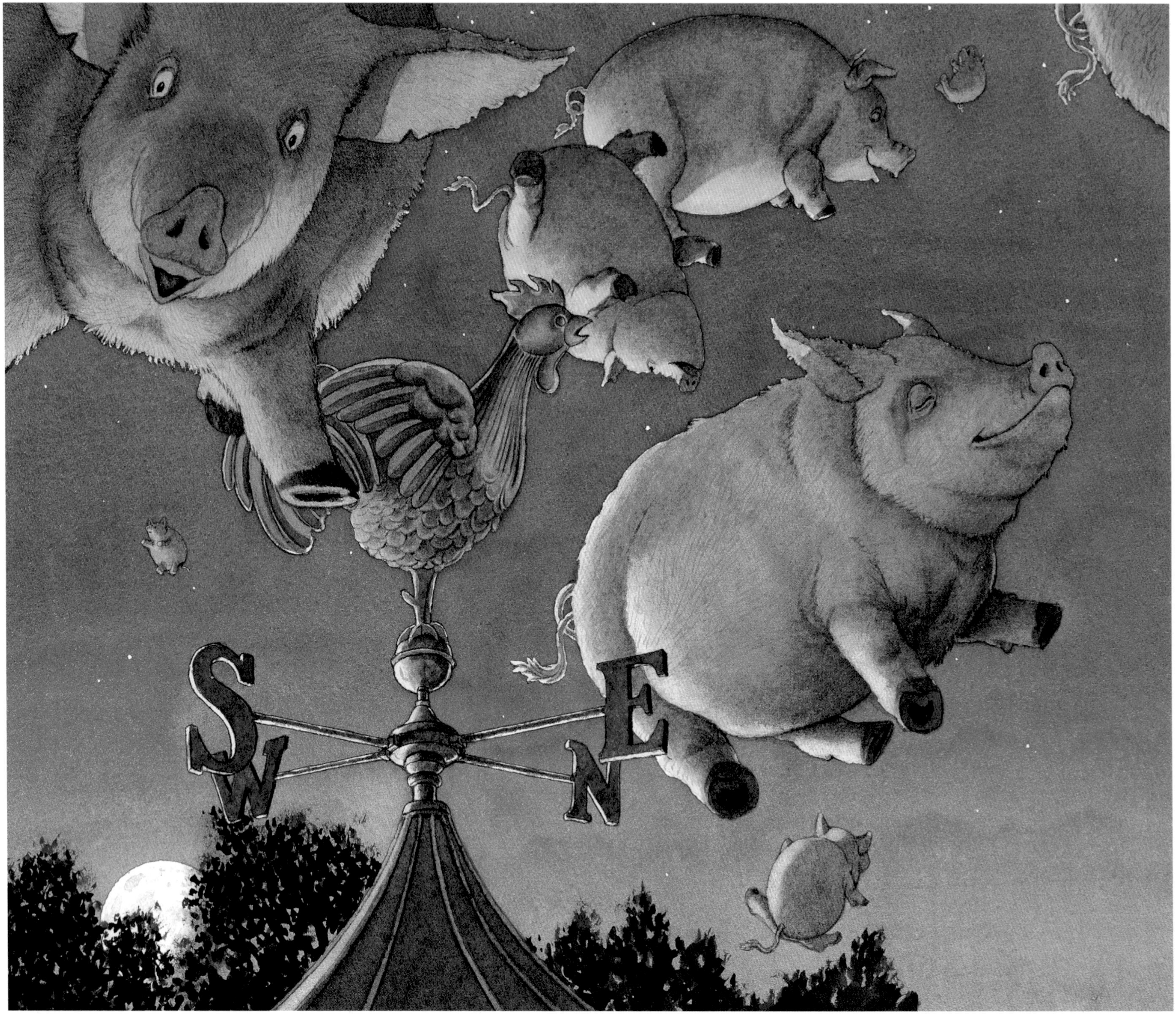
S
W
E
N